COURAGE in TESCO

First published in Great Britain by Hamish Hamilton
Children's Books in 1987
First published in Picture Lions 1989
This edition published in 1992
Picture Lions is an imprint of the Children's Division,
part of HarperCollins Publishers Limited,
77-85 Fulham Palace Road, Hammersmith,
London W6 8JB

Copyright © Babette Cole 1987

The author asserts the moral right to be identified as the
author of the work.

ISBN: 0 00 662964-4

Printed in Great Britain

PictureLions

An Imprint of HarperCollins*Publishers*

Prince Cinders

by
Babette Cole

Prince Cinders was not much of a prince.
He was small, spotty, scruffy and skinny.

He had three big hairy brothers who were always teasing him about his looks.

They spent their time going to the Palace Disco
with princess girlfriends.

They made poor Prince Cinders stay behind and clean up after them.

When his work was done he would sit by the fire
and wish he was big and hairy like his brothers.

One Saturday night, when he was washing the socks, a dirty fairy fell down the chimney.

"All your wishes shall be granted,"
cried the fairy.
"Ziz Ziz Boom, Tic Tac Ta,
This empty can shall be a car."

"Bif Bang Bong, Bo Bo Bo, to the disco you shall go!"

"That can't be right!" said the fairy.

"Toe of rat and eye of newt,
your rags will turn into a suit!"

("Crumbs," thought the fairy,
"I didn't mean a SWIM suit!")

"Your greatest wish I'll grant to you. You SHALL be big and hairy too!"

Prince Cinders got
big and hairy
all right!

"Rats!" said the fairy.
"Wrong again, but I'm sure
it all wears off at midnight."

Prince Cinders didn't know he was a big hairy monkey because that's the kind of spell it was.

He thought he looked pretty good!

So off he went to the disco. The car was too small to drive but he made the best of it.

But when he arrived at the royal Rave up,

he was too big to fit through the door!

He decided to take the bus home.
A pretty princess was waiting at the stop.

"When's the next bus?" he grunted.

Luckily, midnight struck and
Prince Cinders changed back
into himself.

DOING

BUS STOP

The princess thought he had saved her by
frightening away the big hairy monkey!

"Wait!" she shouted, but Prince Cinders was
too shy. He even lost his trousers in the rush!

The princess was none other than the rich and beautiful Princess Lovelypenny. She put out a proclamation to find the owner of the trousers.

Every prince for miles around tried to force the trousers on.

But they wriggled about and refused to fit any of them!

Of course Prince Cinders' brothers all fought to get into the trousers at once. . . .

"Let him try," commanded the princess, pointing at Cinders.

So Prince Cinders married Princess Lovelypenny and lived in luxury, happily ever after. . .